AULOS ®

DESCANT RECORDER TUTOR

TREVOR TREBLE

DEBBIE DESCANT

The Aulos Kids!

© 1980 Chappell Music Ltd
International Music Publications Limited
Griffin House 161 Hammersmith Road
London W6 8BS England

AULOS®

DESCANT RECORDER TUTOR

Standards in recorder playing in schools have never been better.

The AULOS recorder tutor is one of the classic school recorder books. This well loved introduction to recorder playing is suitable for class work or individual study.

The book was specifically commissioned by Chappell to compliment Aulos, the world's most popular recorder.

For three generations Aulos recorders have been used worldwide by more than 75 million children, they are *the* most widely used instruments in our schools today.

This new look tutor will appeal to all current students at Key Stages 1, 2 and 3.

THE AULOS® KIDS
DO's & DON'Ts
OF RECORDER PLAYING

DO BLOW IN TUNE, TONGUE CORRECTLY

DON'T USE LAZY FINGERING

DO STAND OR SIT UP STRAIGHT

DON'T OVERBLOW

DO GREASE THE JOINTS REGULARLY

DON'T EAT BEFORE YOU PLAY

DO LISTEN TO YOUR TEACHER

DON'T CHEW THE MOUTHPIECE

DO KEEP YOUR RECORDER CLEAN

DON'T SHARE YOUR RECORDER

Ideal for Key Stage 1,2 & 3

The Stave and Treble Clef

Music is written on a framework of lines and spaces called a stave.

The Stave

Treble Clef

Notes are written on the lines:

1st line   2nd line   4th line   3rd line   5th line

and in the spaces between the lines:

1st space   3rd space   4th space   2nd space

NOTE VALUES

The Crotchet

A note written like this ♩ or 𝅘𝅥 is called a crotchet, and is worth one beat. The following clapping exercise shows a series of eight crotchets. Clap them evenly like a clock ticking, at the same time counting the beats aloud.

Now the same eight crotchets divided into two groups of four. Clap and count aloud.

The Minim

This note ♩ (or 𝅗𝅥) is called a minim. It is worth two beats. Clap the following exercise making sure you count in a steady pulse.

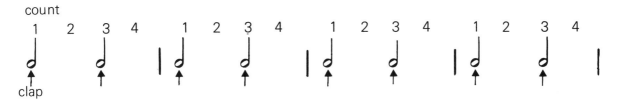

Here are some exercises containing both crotchets ♩ and minims ♩ Keep counting steadily and clap each note.

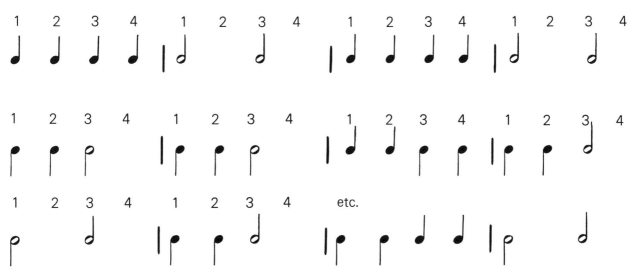

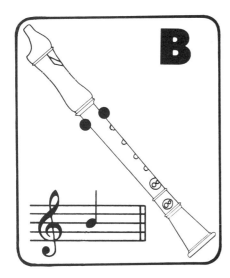

B Playing B

In the diagram, the holes to be covered are shown like this ●

LEFT HAND
Thumb covers the hole at the back, nearest to the mouthpiece.

First finger covers the top hole opposite the thumb. Keep the finger flat so that the pad, rather than the tip is used.

RIGHT HAND
Thumb supports the instrument underneath, at a point roughly opposite the middle hole. The fingers are not used yet.

Place the tip of the recorder between your lips and blow gently. Try to keep the air stream flowing evenly so that the note doesn't waver.

Next, play a series of B's starting each note with a tongue movement as if you were saying 't'. This is known as tonguing and is important because it helps to produce a clean, crisp sound.

Now try the following exercises.

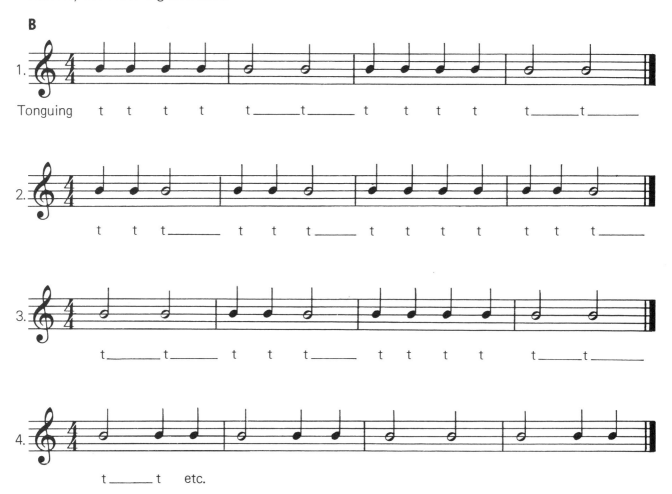

The short upright lines crossing the stave are called bar-lines; they divide the music into measures or bars. A double line is used at the end of a piece.

The $\frac{4}{4}$ sign at the beginning means that each bar contains four crotchets or their equivalent. It is called a time signature.

Playing A

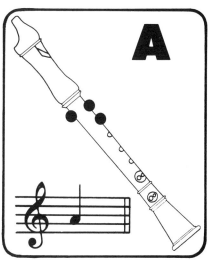

LEFT HAND
Thumb covers the hole at the back. First finger on the first hole and second finger on the second hole.

RIGHT HAND
Thumb supporting as for the note B.
Blow gently and don't forget to tongue each note.

A

Playing A and B

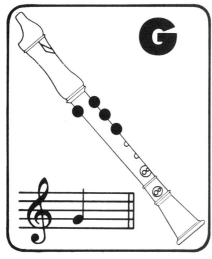

Playing G

LEFT HAND
Thumb, first and second fingers as for the note A. The third finger covers the third hole.

RIGHT HAND
Thumb still supporting.

G

Playing A and G

Playing B, A and G

The Semibreve

The semibreve ○ is a note worth four beats. The following exercises will help you to count it correctly.

Clap and Count

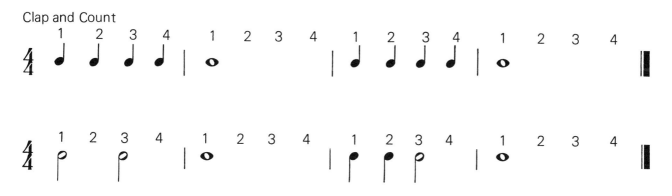

Now play these exercises, being extra careful to keep a steady breath pressure through the semibreve.

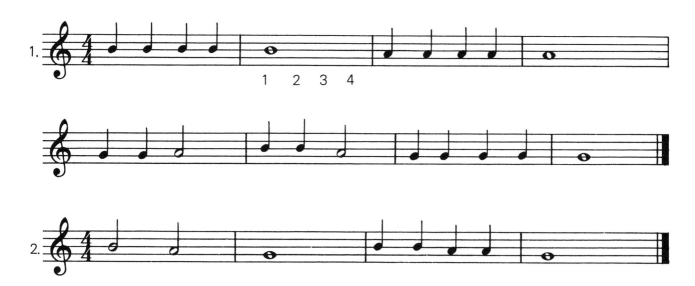

10

Merrily We Roll Along

Suo Gan

Repeat the music between these signs.

Au Clair de la Lune

Repeat

Blow Thy Horn Hunter

Ballade du petit Jesus

De Bretagne

Playing C

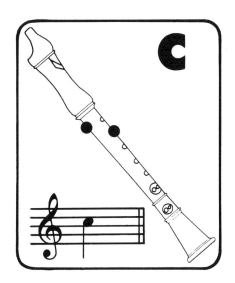

LEFT HAND
Thumb covers the hole at the back. Second finger covers the second hole.
Notice the first hole is NOT covered

RIGHT HAND
Thumb supporting.

✔ This sign means take a breath. Try to make it last until the next breath mark.

C

Playing C and B

Dodo l'enfant do

Playing D

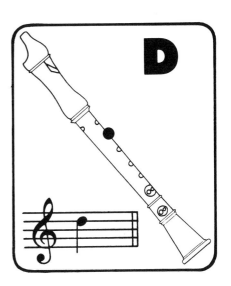

LEFT HAND
Thumbs OFF. Second finger on second hole.

RIGHT HAND
Thumbs supporting

D

1.

2.

Go And Tell Aunt Nancy

Now The Day Is Over

German Folk Song

A New Time Signature

So far all the tunes you have played have been in $\frac{4}{4}$ time i.e. four **crotchet** beats in a bar. Music with three crotchet beats to the bar requires a $\frac{3}{4}$ time signature.

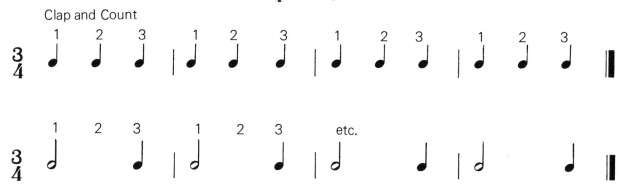

The Dotted Mimim

A minim with a dot after it ♩. is worth three beats, it is known as a dotted mimim.

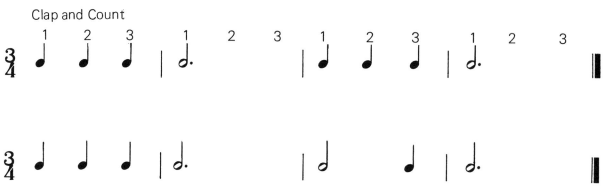

The Quaver

The quaver ♪ is worth half the value of the crotchet so there are two quavers ♫ in one beat. The easiest way to count a series of quavers is like this:

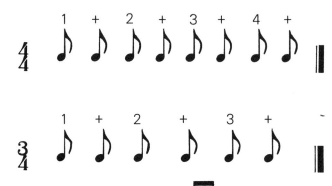

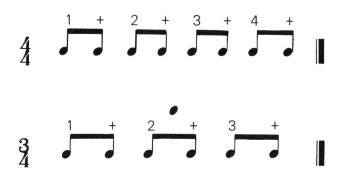

Two quavers are normally joined together like this· ♫ which makes them easier to read.

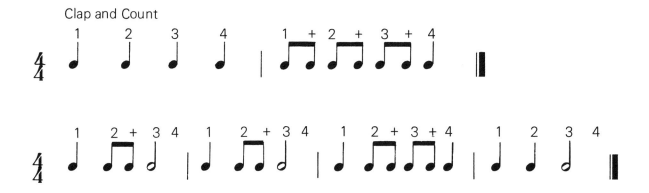

Clap and Count

Pease Pudding Hot

French Folk Song

Summer Goodbye

J'ai Du Bon Tabac

D.C. (Da Cap) al Fine means "Repeat from the beginning to the word 'Fine' (finish)".

Not all tunes begin on the first beat of the bar. Check the time signature and make sure you start counting on the right beat.

I Love Little Pussy

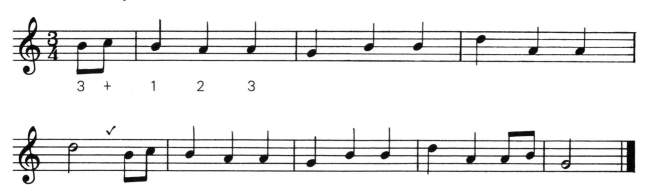

La Chasse.   Paganini

The Crotchet Rest

 This is a Crotchet Rest. It means silence for one beat.

Branle de Sabots   Arbeau

Silesian Folk Song

Playing low D

LEFT HAND
Thumb, first, second and third fingers as for G.
THE LEFT HAND LITTLE FINGER IS NOT USED.

RIGHT HAND
First, second and third fingers covering the next three holes.
Note third finger completely covers double hole.

Blow and tongue very gently and make certain all the holes are
properly covered.

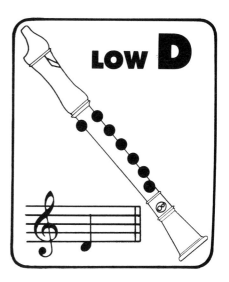

Low D

Westminster Chimes

London's Burning

20

Hot Cross Buns

is another way of grouping four quavers.

Slurred Notes

The slur is a curved line enclosing two or more notes. Slurred notes are to be played "legato" — smoothly without a break in the sound. On the recorder this is achieved by tonguing only the first note and letting the breath continue for the remaining slurred notes.

Sur Le Pont De Nantes

Go From My Window Now

Playing E

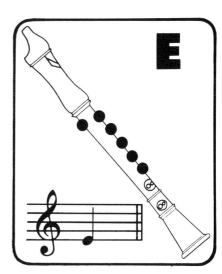

LEFT HAND
Thumb and fingers cover holes as for G.

RIGHT HAND
First finger on first hole, second finger on second hole.

Chinese Folk Song

The Waits

Israeli Folk Song

 Time Signature. Count two beats to the bar.

Volga Boatmen's Song

Gypsy Rover

Old Macdonald Had A Farm

Fine

D.C. al Fine

Tied Notes

The tie is a curved line joining two notes at the same "pitch" (position on the stave). The first note is played and contined without a break into the second.

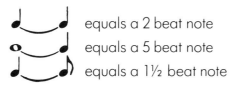

equals a 2 beat note

equals a 5 beat note

equals a 1½ beat note

The Shepherdess

Play   hold

t

Playing F# (F SHARP)

LEFT HAND
Thumb and fingers cover holes as for G.

RIGHT HAND
First hole UNCOVERED. Second finger covers second hole, third finger covers third hole.

The bottom space on this stave is F 🎼 As you know

already the second line is G 🎼 Halfway between the

two (i.e. higher than F but lower than G) is the note called F sharp.

It is shown like this: 🎼

N.B: Notice the sharp sign is placed before the note.

Youth's The Season

Grandmother's Minuet.   Grieg

When a bar contains more than one F sharp, the ♯ sign is only placed before the first F.

I Have Been A Forester

Key Signature

Normally when F sharp recurs throughout a tune, it is shown by a "key signature" at the beginning of each line of music.

The sign is placed on the top line of the stave (this line is also an F) like this:

With this key signature, all the F's in the music become F♯, so a tune written like this

would be played

A key signature can contain more than one sharp i.e.

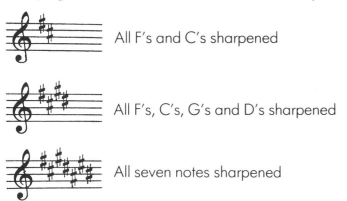 All F's and C's sharpened

All F's, C's, G's and D's sharpened

All seven notes sharpened

More tunes containing F sharp.

Bobby Shaftoe

In der Wiegen

Oh No John

Dotted Crotchet and Quaver Rhythm ♩. ♪

The sound of this rhythmic figure is familiar to everyone, as it occurs in many well known tunes:

You will notice the dotted crotchet ♩. is held longer than the ordinary crotchet, and in each case is followed by the short quaver ♪

The following exercises will help you to count **this** rhythmic figure correctly.

Clap and count, repeating several times.

Now the same exercise but with the crotchet and first quaver tied. You still count "one two and", but miss the clap on the tied quaver.

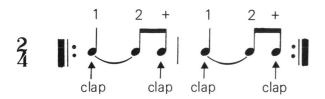

is equal in value to a dotted crotchet ♩. so the exercise you have just clapped can be written like this:

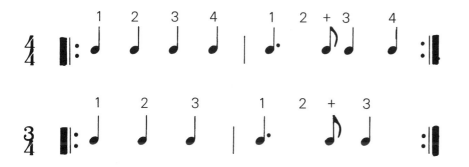

Now clap and count the following exercises, repeating several times:

One Man Went To Mow

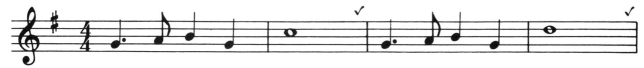

John Come Kiss Me Now

28

Who Liveth So Merry

Colleen

Polish Carol

Quodling's Delight

Skye Boat Song

German Dance   Beethoven

Fine   staccato

D.C. al Fine

A note with a dot above or below, should be played 'staccato' i.e. cut short, detached.
Use your tongue to stop the note as soon as it has sounded.

Basse Dance   Arbeau

The King's Pleasure

Shaker Melody

There Was A Pretty Maid

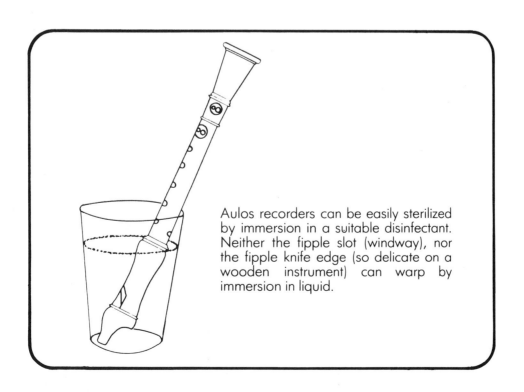

Aulos recorders can be easily sterilized by immersion in a suitable disinfectant. Neither the fipple slot (windway), nor the fipple knife edge (so delicate on a wooden instrument) can warp by immersion in liquid.

Printed by Halstan & Co. Ltd., Amersham, Bucks., England

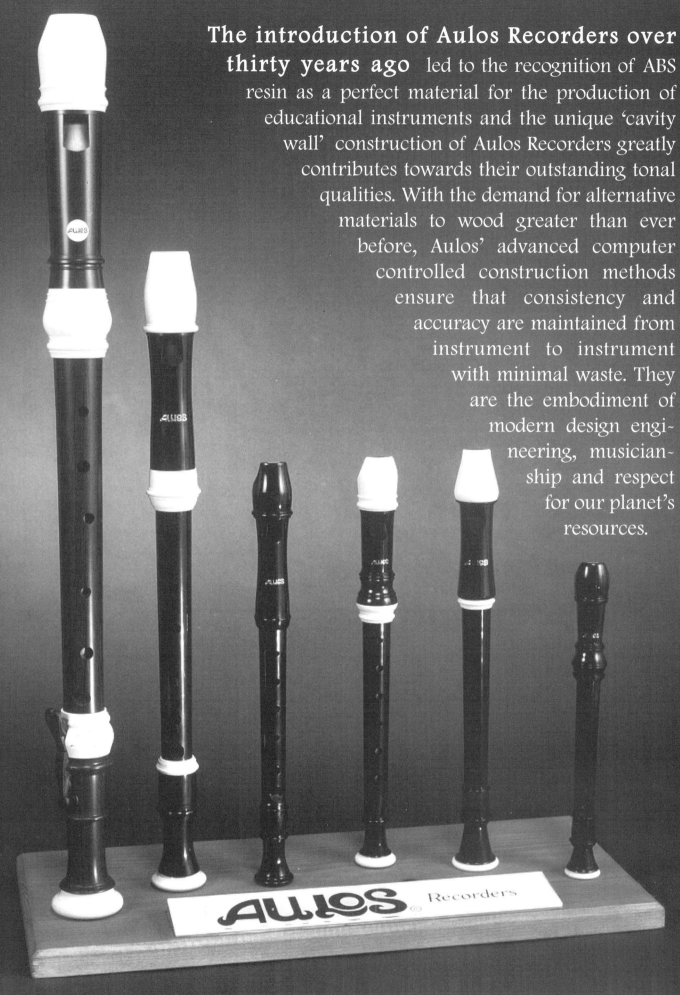

The introduction of Aulos Recorders over thirty years ago led to the recognition of ABS resin as a perfect material for the production of educational instruments and the unique 'cavity wall' construction of Aulos Recorders greatly contributes towards their outstanding tonal qualities. With the demand for alternative materials to wood greater than ever before, Aulos' advanced computer controlled construction methods ensure that consistency and accuracy are maintained from instrument to instrument with minimal waste. They are the embodiment of modern design engineering, musicianship and respect for our planet's resources.

Exclusive UK Distributors, FCN Music • Morley Road • Tonbridge • TN9 1RA • Telephone 01732 366421 • Fax 01732 350367